T0167650

FOLK TALES FOR

Bold Girls

FOLK TALES FOR

Bold Girls

Fiona Collins

ILLUSTRATIONS BY
ED FISHER

The
History
Press

This book is for Sydney Archer,
and all the other bold girls like her.

First published 2019

The History Press
97 St George's Place, Cheltenham
Glos, GL50 3QB
www.thehistorypress.co.uk

© Fiona Collins, 2019

The right of Fiona Collins to be identified as the Author
of this work has been asserted in accordance with the
Copyright, Designs and Patents Act 1988.

British Library Cataloguing in Publication Data.
A catalogue record for this book is available from the British Library.

ISBN 978 0 7509 9049 3

Typesetting and origination by The History Press
Printed and bound in Great Britain by TJ International Ltd.

Contents

Acknowledgements

Ed and I would like to say thank you to all the bold girls who posed for the pictures in this book: Amber, Amy, Bella, Bronwen, Chloe, Dylan, Florence, Freya, Holly, Lois, Lucy, Mabel, Tiana and Tiahna.

Diolch yn fawr / thank you to my friends in Mrs Mollison-White's class at Ysgol Carrog, our village school, for reading the stories and telling me what they thought of them. Here are some of their comments:

Bethan said, 'I love the book: it is very adventurous.'

Callum thought, 'It's a good way to tell stories that you might not find in other places.'

Corey's advice was: 'It was really fun. I'd recommend buying it for people my age.'

Florence thought it was easy to read, but not too easy, and Holly said, 'It wasn't too long.'

Ben said, 'It's a really nice book', and Dylan said, 'It's amazing!'

Thank you to storytellers Mary Medlicott and Betty Rosen, two of my dearest storytelling teachers, who were kind enough to send me their thoughts about the stories, and to Nicola Guy at The History Press, who liked the idea of a book of *Folk Tales for Bold Girls* enough to say, 'Go ahead and do it!'

I also want to thank Sydney Archer, a real-life bold girl, who lives in England and is 7 years old in 2019. Her Aunt Jane won the chance to have this book dedicated to Sydney at a Promises Auction in support of Conwy Arts Trust, here in North Wales, where I live. Sydney, I hope you like your book.

Finally, and most of all, thank you to all the storytellers who first told the stories I have chosen for this book. Some of them were told to me by people I know, and some I first found in other storytellers' books, and worked out my own way to tell them. I would like to say thank you to them all, for sharing the stories, and keeping them alive and on the wind.

And thank you, dear reader, for choosing to read them! I hope you like them, especially if you are a bold girl too.

Introduction

I have chosen some of my favourite bold girl stories for this book, but I couldn't fit all of them into one collection. There are stories here about bold girls from many different countries, but, of course, these are only a few of the tales that are told all around the world. All the stories in this book come from countries that are north of the equator, but that doesn't mean there aren't any bold girl stories in the southern hemisphere; we need a second bold girls book, full of southern stories.

If you like the stories you find here, please tell them. Don't worry about telling them in my words. Tell them in your own way! That's how stories go all around the world.

The Girl
Who Found
the Stories

A TALE FROM THE FIRST
NATION PEOPLE OF AMERICA

In the long, long, long ago days, before there were shops, before there were farms, and before people had learned how to grow food, the only way to get food was by hunting. If you had a good hunter in your family, you would be sleek and healthy, and if you didn't have a good hunter, you'd be weak, and you'd get sick easily, because it's hard to keep healthy when you don't have enough to eat.

But this is the story of a family where there was a good hunter. It was a family of three people: a mother, a daughter and a son. I don't know what had happened to the dad. Maybe he went hunting one day and something terrible happened, and he never came back ...

The son was only little, around four years old. He was too young to be a hunter. But the daughter was nine, and she was already a good hunter. She made herself a bow and arrows, and every day she would go hunting for birds to feed her family.

On the day when the story begins, the girl was hunting. She shot six or seven birds; they fell from the sky and she tied them to her belt. As she went through the forest, she came to a clearing in the trees, where a stream sparkled in the sunlight. Next to the stream was a great flat stone. The girl looked at the stone and she thought, 'I bet that stone is warm from the sun.'

She put her hand on the stone and it was warm. She thought: 'I could sit here for a while and rest. I've got plenty of birds: I can rest for a bit.'

So she climbed up and sat on the great stone. She put down her bow and arrows. She untied the birds from her belt and put them beside her. She stretched out her legs on the warm stone. She turned up her face to the sun. It was warm too. It was so peaceful there that she almost fell asleep.

Then, suddenly, she heard a voice.

'Would you like me to tell you a story?'

She snapped her eyes open and looked around, but she couldn't see anyone. 'Who's talking to me?'

'I'm talking to you.' The voice was coming from underneath her.

She looked down at the stone, and said, 'Are you talking to me?'

The stone said, 'Yes, it's me: I'm talking to you. Would you like me to tell you a story?'

The girl said, 'What's a story?'

Because this story comes from so long ago that stories had not even been invented.

The stone said, 'Stories are the things that people tell each other to remember the past, and to dream about the future, to teach people good ways to live and to explain why the world is the way it is. Would you like me to tell you a story?'

The girl said, 'Oh, yes please, I think I would like to have a story.'

'Well,' said the stone, 'if I give you a story, what will you give me in return?'

The girl thought about this. She didn't have any presents with her. She looked at her bow and arrows, but she thought: 'I can't give the stone my weapons, I need them to get food for the family.'

She looked at her clothes, but she thought: 'I can't give the stone my clothes, they're all much too scruffy.'

Then she looked at the dead birds, and she thought: 'I could give the stone these birds. I can hunt again to get more for the family.'

So she said to the stone, 'Would you like me to give you the birds?'

The stone replied, 'Thank you. That will do nicely.'

And then it seemed as though the sunlight shimmered and shone more brightly. Those still birds stirred, their stiff feathers softened, their dull eyes brightened, their dead beaks opened, their chests began to rise and fall … until they spread their wings and, with a *swooooosh* … they flew away into the sky.

When the birds had disappeared from sight, the stone began to tell the girl a story. She listened, and she listened. When that story was finished, the stone told another, and another. The day seemed to go past so quickly that, when the stone stopped for a moment, and the girl looked at the sky, she was surprised to see that the sun was low in the west.

'Oh, it's getting late!' she said. 'Soon it will be dark. I must go. I must get food for my family.' She jumped down from the stone. 'Thank you for the stories. Can I come again tomorrow for some more?'

'Yes, you can,' said the stone.

She grabbed her bow and arrows and started to run home. As she ran she was looking for birds to hunt. But it was getting late. She was going home; the birds were going to their nests. She saw one bird and shot it, then one more, but when she got home she only had two small birds to give to her mother.

Her mother was worried. 'What's happened to the hunting?' she asked. 'Where are all the birds?'

The girl didn't want to tell her mother about the stone. She wanted to keep it a secret. So she said, 'Oh, there just weren't many birds around today, mum.'

The mother, the brother and the girl shared the two little birds. They were still hungry when they went to bed. It's hard to sleep when you are hungry. The mum couldn't sleep at all. She was thinking: 'What's happened to the hunting? Where are all the birds? How can I feed the family?'

Next morning the girl went out hunting again. The mum called her son to her. He was only little. He was too young to be a hunter. But he was already a good tracker.

She said to him, 'Follow your sister. Watch where she goes. Keep her in your sight, but keep out of her sight. Find out what's happened to the hunting. Find out, where are all the birds?'

So, as the girl went through the forest, her brother followed her. He hid behind a tree and watched her. Then he ran to another tree and hid again, always keeping her in sight, always keeping out of her sight.

He followed her through the forest. He watched her shooting birds and tying them to her belt. Soon she had seven or eight dead birds. He followed her to a clearing in the trees, where a stream sparkled in the sunlight. Next to the stream was a great flat stone.

He watched her go across the clearing, but he couldn't follow her, because there were no trees for him to hide behind. He had to stay at the edge and watch. He saw her go to the stone and sit on it. He could see that she was talking to someone, but there was no one else there. Then he saw the dead birds come to life and fly away! And then he could see that she was listening to something, but he was too far away to hear what she was listening to. So he went a bit nearer, and a bit nearer, and a bit nearer, till there were two of them sitting on the stone, listening to the stories.

All that day, the sister and the brother sat on the stone listening to stories, until it was too late to do much hunting.

When they came home with just one bird, their mother asked, 'What's happened to the hunting? Where are all the birds?'

The girl and her brother looked at each other. They wanted to keep the stone a secret. They just said, 'Oh, there weren't many birds around today, mum.'

So the next day, the mother sent their cousin to track them ... and so there were three of them, sitting on the stone all day, listening to stories.

The next day, there were more people there. The day after, even more, until everyone was there, children and grown-ups, day after day, listening to stories.

Until one day, the stone finished a story and it stopped.

The people said, 'Tell us another one. It isn't very late. There's time for one more …'

But the stone said: 'No, I can't. I've told you all my stories. Now you must be the ones to tell them.'

And with a crack and a crunch and a rumble and a roll, the stone fell into a thousand pieces.

The people stood and stared, and then, slowly, one by one, each of them came forward and picked up a piece of the stone. Some people chose a small stone, and some a big one. Some people chose a stone because they liked its shape, and some because they liked the colour. Each one chose a piece of the stone to keep, to remember the stone that had told the stories. And they remembered what the stone had told them, that now they had the stories and they must be the ones to tell them.

Some people remembered all the stories they had heard, and they told them to everyone they met.

Some people just remembered a few of the stories, but they told them to everyone they met.

Some people only remembered one story, their favourite story, but they told it over and over again until they got really good at telling it.

And some people couldn't remember any of the stories at all, they only remembered they had been somewhere and listened to stories, so they made that into a story.

And my friend June heard that story from our friend Tony.

She told it to me.

Now I've told it to you.

If you tell the story to someone you know, it will never be forgotten.

That's how stories go all around the world.

Tipingi

A TALE FROM HAITI, IN THE CARIBBEAN

Once there was a little girl called Tipingi (*you say it like this: tip-in-gee, as if you were going to say 'geese'*). Tipingi lived in a house that had belonged to her father. Her father was no longer there. I don't know what had happened to him.

Tipingi lived with a woman who treated her like a servant, even though the house belonged to Tipingi now. She wouldn't let Tipingi invite friends round, and she made her do all the work when she came home from school.

One day, when Tipingi was at school, the woman was cooking sweets to sell in the market. The fire under her cooking pot went out. Usually, she would have sent Tipingi to get firewood, but Tipingi wasn't there, so she had to go herself.

She walked into the forest and found some wood. Being greedy, she gathered a great big pile. But the pile was too heavy for her to carry. She tried this way and she tried that way, but she couldn't lift it all up. At last, she shouted out, 'My friends, I have a big pile of firewood, but it is too heavy for me to carry home. Will someone help me carry my wood?'

An old man came through the trees. He said, 'I will help you carry your wood. But how will you pay me?'

The woman said, 'I will find something in my house to give you.'

So the old man carried the wood.

When they got to the house he said, 'I have carried your wood. Now, what will you give me?'

And the woman replied, 'There's a girl who lives here, called Tipingi. I will give her to you, to be your servant.'

Now Tipingi was just coming home from school, and when she heard her name she stepped out of sight and listened hard.

The woman said, 'Tomorrow, when I send the girl to school, I will make sure she is wearing a blue shirt. Wait for her at the end of the day. When you see the girl with the blue shirt, call her by her name, Tipingi, and she will come to you. Then you can take her.'

Tipingi thought, 'Oh no he can't!' She ran to the homes of the people in her class, and said to them, 'Please help me. Come to school tomorrow wearing a blue shirt.'

The next day at hometime, the old man was waiting outside the school. He saw a girl wearing a blue shirt. He saw a boy wearing a blue shirt. Then he saw another girl. Her shirt was blue too.

'Which one of you is Tipingi?' he asked.

'I'm Tipingi,' said the first girl.

'She's Tipingi,' said the boy.

'We're Tipingi too,' said the second girl.

Then they began to jump up and down and sing:

I'm Tipingi
She's Tipingi
We're Tipingi too.

The old man said 'Bah!'

He went back to the woman and said, 'I waited by the school, but all the children were wearing blue and they all said they were Tipingi. You tricked me.'

'No,' said the woman. 'It must be a mistake. Tomorrow I will send her to school with her red dress on. You will find her. The one with a red dress will be Tipingi.'

But Tipingi heard what the woman said, and she ran to her friends' houses and asked them to help her again.

The next day the old man went back to the school. He saw a girl wearing a red dress. He saw a boy wearing a red dress. He saw another girl wearing a red dress. They were all wearing red dresses!

'Which one of you is Tipingi?' he asked.

'I'm Tipingi,' said the first girl.

'She's Tipingi,' said the boy.

'We're Tipingi too,' said the second girl.

Then they began to twirl round and round and sing:

I'm Tipingi
She's Tipingi
We're Tipingi too.

The old man said 'Ugh!'

He went back to the woman and said, 'I waited by the school, but all the children were wearing red and they all said they were Tipingi. You tricked me.'

'No,' said the woman. 'It must be a mistake. Tomorrow I will send her to school with her green shorts on. You will find her. The one wearing green shorts will be Tipingi.'

But Tipingi heard what the woman said, and she ran to her friends' houses and asked them for help again.

The next day the old man was back at the school. He saw a boy wearing green shorts.

He saw another boy wearing green shorts.
He saw a girl wearing green shorts. They
were all wearing green shorts!

'Which one of you is Tipingi?' he asked.

'I'm Tipingi,' said the first boy.

'She's Tipingi,' said the other boy.

'We're all Tipingi!' said the girl.

Then they began to dance in a ring and
sing:

I'm Tipingi
She's Tipingi
We're Tipingi too.

The old man said 'Agh!'

He went back to the woman. He said, 'I
waited by the school, but all the children
were wearing green shorts and they all said
they were Tipingi. I don't believe you have
a girl to be my servant. You are just trying
to trick me. I need a servant. I'll take you!'

When Tipingi came home from school,
the woman was gone.

From then on, Tipingi lived peacefully in her own house, with no one to tell her what to do. Her friends came round whenever she invited them, and they all wore whatever colour they liked!

The Girl Who Wasn't Afraid

A TALE FROM IRELAND

In Ireland, in the old days, people used to say that you must never leave dirty water in your house overnight. When you washed your feet before you went to bed, you had to empty the bowl out of the back door before you went upstairs, otherwise all kinds of creatures and spirits might come in. This story is about what happened when a family forgot to do this.

An old woman and her daughter lived in a lonely sort of place, and one night they forgot to throw out the feet water. They hadn't been in bed very long, when they heard footsteps in the yard and a knocking at the door. Then a voice called out, 'Key, key, let us in.'

The old woman didn't answer, nor did her daughter.

But the key did! It said, 'I can't let you in. I am tied to the post at the bottom of the old woman's bed.'

Then the voice called out, 'Feet water, feet water, let us in.'

The bowl of dirty water tipped over. The water ran across the kitchen floor and the back door opened, letting the water out. And letting the strangers in …

A woman came in. She had a green face and a horn on her head. Behind her there was another woman with a green face. She had two horns on her head. There was another green-faced woman behind them. She had three horns on her head …

Seven women came in, one behind the other. Each had a green face. Each had more horns on her head than the one before: the last woman had seven horns.

The girl got quietly out of her bed, hid at the top of the stairs and watched the strangers. Each one had a bag and each one had a spinning wheel. They sat down, took wool out of the bags and began to spin it into thread.

This went on for a couple of hours, and the girl's mother was shaking with fright.

'When they have finished spinning, what are they going to do?' she whispered to her daughter.

'Don't worry, mum,' said the girl, 'I'll get rid of them.' And, bold as brass, she went down the stairs and picked up the bucket. 'You must be getting thirsty with all this spinning,' she said. 'I'll go to the well for some water and make you all a cup of tea.'

She went out of the kitchen to the well. But she didn't fill her bucket. She put it down and ran as fast as she could to the wise woman's house. She knocked on the door. When the wise woman opened it, she quickly explained what had happened.

'It's lucky you've come to me,' said the wise woman, 'because I know who they are. They come from the wild mountain. I can tell you what to do to get rid of them, but you must throw out the feet water as soon as they have gone, or it will let them back in!'

And she told the girl what to do.

The girl thanked her, and back she went to the well, as fast as she could go. When she got there, she shouted at the top of her voice, 'The wild mountain is on fire, and all the air above it!'

The door banged open, and the seven women came running out screaming.

As the girl watched, they rose up into the air and flew away towards the wild mountain. Straight away, she rushed indoors, threw their spinning wheels and bags of wool into the yard and swept out the feet water from the floor. Then she locked the door, and she and her mother went back to bed.

It wasn't long before they heard footsteps in the yard again, and a voice called out, 'Key, key, let us in.'

But the key said, 'How can I? I told you, I am tied to the post at the bottom of the old woman's bed.'

Then the voice called out, 'Feet water, feet water, let us in.'

The feet water said, 'How can I? I'm out here with you, under your feet.'

The women shouted and yelled, but they couldn't get in. They had no power now the feet water had been thrown out. At last, they picked up their spinning wheels and bags and flew away, back to the wild mountain.

From then on, you can be sure that the girl and her mother always threw out the feet water and tidied everything up before they locked the door and went to bed each night.

Molly Whuppie

A TALE FROM SCOTLAND

Once upon a time there were three sisters, and their names were Milly, Polly and Molly Whuppie. Even though Molly was the youngest, she was the boldest.

One day, their parents took them into the wood and left them there! (*Don't let your parents do this: it's a very bad idea, and if they do it, they will feel really sorry afterwards ...*)

Milly and Polly cried and cried, but Molly said, 'Let's go out into the world to seek our fortunes!' So they walked and walked until they came to the edge of the wood, and they saw a great grey castle. Molly went straight to the front door and knocked.

A little old woman opened the door.

'Excuse me,' said Molly, politely. 'We are three sisters and we are lost in the woods. We are very tired, and hungry and thirsty. Please could we come in to have a little rest, and maybe something to eat and drink?'

The old woman replied, 'Well, you're welcome to come in, my dears, but I live here with my son, and he's a giant. He has a great big bommieknocker for bashing people with. If he comes home while you are here, he is sure to bop each one of you with his bommieknocker and eat you all up.'

'If we go before he comes home, can we come in?' asked Molly. 'We are really tired from all the walking.'

'Well, all right then,' said the old woman, and she let them in.

The girls went into the kitchen, and the old woman gave them some bread and milk. Before they had finished, they heard the front door slam, and very heavy footsteps coming down the corridor to the kitchen. They didn't have time to run away. They didn't have time to hide …

Then they heard something else. It was the voice of the giant. He was saying what giants always say:

Fee, fi, fo, fum,
I smell the blood of an Englishman.
Be he alive, or be he dead,
I'll grind his bones to make my bread!

In came the giant. He was big. Bigger than big. He was carrying a great big stick. The girls knew this was his terrible bommieknocker. He said, 'I'm hungry and I'm thirsty, Mum.'

His mother quickly filled a bucket with milk for him. He drank it all in one gulp. She stuck two loaves of bread together with butter and cheese and gave him his sandwich. He ate it in two bites. He was still hungry. He looked at the girls.

'Hello, Mr Giant,' said Molly, quickly. 'How nice to meet you. It's lucky that you aren't going to eat us.'

'Aren't I?' asked the giant.

'Oh no,' said Molly. 'You see, we aren't men, we're girls, and we aren't English, we're Scottish. So that's all right, isn't it?'

The giant didn't know what to say. But he was still hungry, so he thought of a plan.

'It will soon be dark,' he said. 'Why don't you stay the night here?'

Molly didn't think it was a good idea, but her sisters did. They were very tired. Soon they were all tucked up in three little beds in the spare room. But Molly still didn't think it was a good idea, and she made her sisters hide under the beds. She put pillows under the bedclothes so it looked as though they were all asleep in their beds. Then she crawled under her bed and hid too.

Just in time!

The bedroom door opened and the giant crept in. He was carrying his great big bommieknocker.

He patted Milly's bed until he felt the shape of the pillow. 'There you are,' he whispered, 'and here you are!' And he bopped the bed with his great big bommieknocker!

He patted Polly's bed until he felt the shape of the pillow. 'There you are,' he whispered, 'and here you are!' And he bopped the bed with his great big bommieknocker!

He did the same to Molly's bed too, and then he laughed a horrible laugh. 'In the morning, I shall have smashed little girls on toast for breakfast,' he said. And off he went to bed.

As soon as he had gone, Molly called her sisters out from under the beds. She led them out of the bedroom and along the corridors of the giant's castle, until they came to the front door. They let themselves out very quietly, and ran away through the forest as fast as they could. They ran and they ran until they came to a deep, steep valley.

There was a bridge across the valley, made of one hair. They ran across the Bridge of One Hair and so they came safely to another kingdom.

Soon they saw another great grey castle. Molly went straight to the front door and knocked.

A king opened the door.

'Excuse me,' said Molly, politely. 'We are three sisters and we've come a long way. We are looking for work. Have you got any jobs we can do?'

'Where have you come from?' asked the king.

'We've come across the Bridge of One Hair,' said Molly.

'Oh no,' said the king, 'you couldn't have come from there. There's a giant there. He eats anyone who goes across the Bridge of One Hair. No one ever comes back.'

'Well, we have,' said Molly.

The king was very impressed. He said they could come to live in the castle and work there.

A few days later, the king said to Molly, 'I've been thinking about the giant. I've heard that he has a great big bommie-knocker. If only there were someone brave enough and bold enough to go over the Bridge of One Hair and take away his great big bommieknocker, he wouldn't be able to hurt people any more.

Molly, I can only think of one person brave enough and bold enough to do it. And that person is Molly Whuppie. Will you go? If you will, I will give you whatever you want.'

'Well,' said Molly, 'I can't really think of anything that I want, and I don't know if I can do it. But I'll try.'

So away she went, over the Bridge of One Hair and through the forest in the dead of night, until she came to the giant's castle.

She crept through the corridors of the castle until she came to the giant's bedroom, and peeped round the door. The giant's bed was in the middle of his room, and he was fast asleep. His head was on his pillow, and leaning against the bed was his great big bommieknocker.

Very quietly, Molly crept into the bedroom.

Very quietly, she picked up the great big bommieknocker.

Very quietly, she crept out of the bedroom.

But just as she went through the door, the bommieknocker tapped against the door post. It only made a little noise, but it woke the giant! He jumped out of bed and he chased her.

So she ran. And he ran.

Molly ran through the corridors of the castle and the giant ran after her. She ran through the forest in the dead of night, and the giant ran after her. She ran until she came to the Bridge of One Hair, and the giant ran after her. She ran across the Bridge of One Hair.

But the giant was too big and too heavy to cross over. He had to stay on his side. He shook his fist and shouted, 'Molly Whuppie, Molly Whuppie, don't you ever come here again!'

And Molly, on the other side, grinned and waved in a very annoying sort of way, and called out, 'Twice more, my friend, will I come here again.' She took the great big bommieknocker back to the king's castle.

He was delighted. 'Now my people will be safe. Thank you, Molly. What can I give you?'

'I can't think of anything I want,' said Molly, 'but my sister Milly really likes horses. Maybe you could give her a farm?'

The king was very happy to give Milly a farm, and Milly was very happy with her horses.

Soon the king started thinking about the giant again. He said to Molly, 'I've been thinking about the giant. I've heard that he has a magic purse of gold, and no matter how much money you take out, it is never empty. If only there were someone brave enough and bold enough to go over the Bridge of One Hair and bring me his magic purse of gold, I could buy hospitals and schools and libraries and parks and all the things my people need. Molly, I can only think of one person brave enough and bold enough to do it. And that person is Molly Whuppie. Will you go? If you will, I will give you whatever you want.'

'Well,' said Molly, 'I can't really think of anything that I want, and I don't know if I can do it. But I'll try.'

So away she went, over the Bridge of One Hair and through the forest in the dead of night, until she came to the giant's castle.

She crept through the corridors of the castle until she came to the giant's bedroom, and peeped round the door. The giant's bed was in the middle of his room, and he was fast asleep. His head was on his pillow, and next to his head was his magic purse of gold.

Very quietly, Molly crept into the bedroom.

Very quietly, she picked up the magic purse of gold.

Very quietly, Molly crept out of the bedroom.

But just as she went through the door, the magic purse tapped against the doorframe. It woke the giant! He jumped out of bed and he chased her.

So she ran. And he ran.

Molly ran through the corridors of the castle and the giant ran after her. She ran through the forest in the dead of night, and the giant ran after her. She ran until she came to the Bridge of One Hair, and the giant ran after her. She ran across the Bridge of One Hair.

But the giant was too big and too heavy to cross over. He had to stay on his side. He shook his fist and shouted, 'Molly Whuppie, Molly Whuppie, don't you ever come here again!'

And Molly, on the other side, grinned and waved in a very annoying sort of way, and called out, 'Once more, my friend, will I come here again.' She took the magic purse of gold back to the king's castle.

He was delighted. He used it to buy hospitals and schools and libraries and parks and all the things the people needed.

'Thank you, Molly,' said the king. 'What shall I give you?'

'I can't think of anything I want,' said Molly, 'but my sister Polly really likes clothes. Maybe you could give her a clothes shop?'

The king was very happy to give Polly a shop, and Polly was very happy selling clothes.

Soon the king started thinking about the giant again. He said to Molly, 'I've been thinking about the giant. I've heard that he has a magic wishing ring, and if you are wearing it, whatever you wish for will come true. If only there were someone brave enough and bold enough to go over the Bridge of One Hair and bring me the magic wishing ring, I could wish for everything my people need, and make them happy.

Molly, I can only think of one person brave enough and bold enough to do it. And that person is Molly Whuppie.

Will you go? If you will, I will give you whatever you want.'

'Well,' said Molly, 'I can't really think of anything that I want, and I don't know if I can do it. But I'll try.'

So away she went, over the Bridge of One Hair and through the forest in the dead of night, until she came to the giant's castle.

She crept through the corridors of the castle until she came to the giant's bedroom, and peeped round the door. The giant's bed was in the middle of his room, and he was fast asleep. His head was on his pillow, and his hand was by his head.

His thumb was on his hand. And on his thumb was the magic wishing ring.

Very quietly, Molly crept into the bedroom.

Very quietly, she got hold of the magic wishing ring.

Very carefully, she pulled it off the giant's thumb.

It was too big for her to wear, so she put it over her head and round her waist, like a belt. Then she turned to go out of the bedroom.

But a great big hand grabbed her.

The giant sat up in bed. 'So, Molly Whuppie,' he said. 'I've got you now.'

'Yes,' said Mollie. 'You have.'

'Well, Molly Whuppie,' said the giant, 'if I was Molly Whuppie and you were the giant, what would you do now, eh?'

'If I was the giant and you were Molly Whuppie, I don't know what I would do. But I'm not the giant, I'm Molly Whuppie. And I do know what to do.'

Molly touched the magic wishing ring around her waist and said, 'I wish we were at the Bridge of One Hair!'

In a flash they were there. Molly jumped out of the giant's hand and ran across the bridge.

Even in his pyjamas, the giant was too big and heavy to cross over. He stamped his foot and shook his fist and shouted, 'Molly Whuppie, Molly Whuppie, don't you ever come here again!'

And Molly, on the other side, grinned and waved in a very annoying sort of way, and called out, 'Never more, my friend, will I come here again.'

She took the magic wishing ring back to the king's castle. He was delighted. He used it to wish for everything that was needed to make the people happy.

'Thank you, Molly,' said the king. 'What shall I give you?'

'I can't think of anything I want,' said Molly, 'except that I really like having adventures. Maybe you could make me your Chief Adventurer?'

The king was very happy to make Molly his Chief Adventurer, and Molly was very happy too. She carried on having adventures for the rest of her life. And she never went back over the Bridge of One Hair again.

Seren

A TALE FROM WALES

Seren lived near the River Llugwy (*you say it a bit like this: huh-lig-whee*) in North Wales. Her mother loved to sing, and Seren had a sweet singing voice too. Her father was a blacksmith, and Seren grew up to the sound of her mother's songs, the ringing of her father's hammer on the anvil and the crackle of the fire in the forge.

Everyone got their water and food from the river. There were plenty of fish in the river when Seren was a baby, but as she grew up, things changed: there were fewer and fewer fish in the river for the village people to eat. Something else was eating them. Nobody knew what this new creature in the river was, until it had finished all the fish, and started looking for something else to eat.

When it crawled out of the river, everyone was amazed by its huge size. Then they were horrified, because it struck out with huge claws at the people who were standing near. And then they were terrified, as it dragged two people back into the water to drown them and eat them.

This monster was an afanc (*you say it like this: avank*) with sharp teeth and long claws, thick fur and a broad flat tail. Now, afanc is the Welsh word for 'beaver', and these days beavers are small busy animals which build dams and only eat plants. But this afanc was a monster: as high as a house and as long as a ladder. And once it had decided it liked the taste of humans, life became a nightmare for the people living near the river. Everyone was afraid of being taken by the afanc, and soon everyone knew someone who *had* been taken by the afanc, and never seen again.

Seren's parents stopped letting her go anywhere near the riverbank, even with friends. 'No one will be able to save you if the afanc gets near enough to take you,' they said.

A cold feeling of fear was everywhere.

One day, Seren's mother said, 'We can't go on like this! We don't feel safe in our own place. We need help.'

Seren's father agreed. 'You're right, my love,' he said. 'But who would be brave enough and clever enough and strong enough to get rid of this monster?'

Seren's mother had been thinking about this for a while. 'We need Huw Gadarn,' she said. 'He'll know what to do.'

'Huw Gadarn! Of course! If anyone can help us, it will be Huw,' said Seren's father excitedly. 'That's the first good idea anyone has had since this trouble started.'

Soon Seren's mother's idea was being talked about all around the village, and soon after that, a messenger was sent to find Huw and ask for his help.

Huw Gadarn had come over the sea to bring the first people to Wales, and he was wise, as well as brave and clever and strong. In fact, his name means 'Huw the Mighty'.

When he heard about their troubles, he came at once to help. He brought his two horned oxen with him. They were so big that their horns stretched right across the valley from one side to the other.

Everyone looked at the oxen in surprise. They already had one giant creature … why had Huw brought two more? Then Huw explained. 'My plan is to drag the afanc away from here. Only my oxen are big enough to do that. And only the strongest iron chains will hold the monster. I need all the blacksmiths to make chains from your very best iron. Then they must join all the chains together to make one long strong chain. We'll have to wrap it round the afanc as many times as we can, to keep it from escaping. Then the oxen will pull it far away, so it can't cause any more harm.'

When they heard this, the blacksmiths looked at each other.

Seren's father spoke for them all. 'We can do it! We'll start today!'

Soon all the fires in all the forges of all the blacksmiths were blazing brightly. The whole valley rang to the sound of their hammers beating out hot iron. They shaped rings and linked the rings together.

When the blacksmiths had used up all their iron, they came carrying their chains, clanking and clinking, down the steep paths to the village. Seren's father was waiting, ready to forge the chains together into one long length.

But while the men were busy, Seren's mother was sitting quietly, watching the river in the distance, and thinking. At last, she went to find Huw. 'I understand your plan and it seems like a good one. But how will you get the afanc to come out of the water, and how can you make it wait while you chain it up?'

Huw Gadarn looked at her. 'That is the most difficult and dangerous part of this whole plan,' he said. 'We need to trick the afanc to come out of the water and settle down peacefully. I believe that if someone sits by the river and sings, the afanc will come out to listen. I think the music will calm it, so it will not attack the singer, but I don't know for sure. It's a very dangerous thing to ask someone to do.'

'It certainly is!' said Seren's mother, and she walked away with a worried frown.

Huw Gadarn turned round in surprise when Seren suddenly appeared beside him. 'I heard what you told my mother,' she said. 'I'm a good singer. I'll sing to the afanc on the beach.'

Huw looked at her. She was very young. He opened his mouth to tell her it was too dangerous, but Seren spoke first, with a determined look on her face and her head held up high. 'I'm not scared,' she said. 'Well, yes, I *am* scared, but I know it has to be done and I think I would be a good person to do it!'

Huw stared at her. He changed his mind about what he meant to say. 'Do you know,' he said, slowly, 'I think you might be right. But I don't think your mother will agree …'

Seren's mother said 'No.' She said 'No, no, no!' She told Seren's father to say 'No' too.

But Seren argued with her. 'I *want* to do it. I want to help the village. Everyone says my singing is beautiful. Now here's a chance to make it useful as well!'

Of course, Seren's mother didn't want her to do it. Every mother wants to protect her children. But while they argued, the monster caught and killed three more people. One of them was a little boy who was only four years old. His mother ran along the riverbank crying. 'Can't someone stop this beast before it kills all our children?' she wailed.

Seren looked at her mother. Seren's mother looked at the ground. 'If anything happens to you, I will never forgive myself,' she whispered, and now it was her turn to cry.

Seren went to find Huw. 'What do I need to do?' she asked.

Huw's plan was simple, but he did not know if it would work. He would wait just out of sight, with the horned oxen, the end of the chain looped over their massive shoulders. All the blacksmiths would hide along the riverbank, holding the rest of the long chain ready in their arms, while Seren sat on the beach and sang.

If the afanc heard her, and *if* it liked her song, and *if* it came quietly out of the water, and *if* Seren could persuade it to lie down with its head in her lap, and *if* it went to sleep, the men would rush out and chain it up. Then Huw would get his oxen to pull it far, far away, to somewhere it would not cause any more trouble.

Everyone could see that there were a lot of 'ifs' in Huw's plan, but they trusted him, so they were ready to try it.

Seren sat on the beach and looked at the river. She had known it all her life. But now it was no longer safe for her and her friends.

She wanted to change that. She was scared, but she was bold. She looked around. Her father, holding the long chain, was hiding in the trees. He was the nearest person to her. He had insisted on that. He nodded to her. She nodded back. Everyone was ready; they were all in place.

Seren took a deep breath, and began to sing. At first her voice was wobbly, but soon she relaxed and she began to sing more clearly and strongly. Her voice drifted over the water. It must have drifted under the water, too, because, after a while, she saw bubbles rising in the middle of the river. Then she saw the huge sleek head of the afanc break the surface. It floated there, looking at her, and listening to her song.

Seren gulped with fear when she saw the afanc, but her song only stopped for a moment. She began again, singing about the deep blue water, the soft riverbed. The afanc listened, and swam closer to the shore.

Seren changed to a song about looking at the sky, lying in the sun. She didn't think the afanc could understand the words, but she wanted to do everything she could to make it come out of the water, near enough for her father to catch it.

The monster was crawling up the beach.

She kept singing.

It was close enough for her to smell its wet, slimy coat.

She kept singing.

It was close enough for her to hear it puffing and panting.

She kept singing.

It was close enough for her to feel its breath on her face.

She kept singing.

Very, very slowly, as though it was hard work to move its giant body, it lay down next to her, and put its head in her lap.

Still singing, Seren began to stroke its head, changing the song to a lullaby.

She watched as the afanc's eyes began to close. She realised that her soft song was working: her lullaby was lulling the afanc to sleep.

She kept singing and stroking its head. But she lifted her other hand to signal to her father.

There was a long moment when nothing happened.

Then, suddenly, the men were all around her. The chains were clashing together as they threw them over the monster, which was roaring and thrashing around. Her father grabbed Seren from behind and pulled her out from under the afanc. As he did so, it lashed out with its long sharp claws. Seren felt a horrible pain in her chest. She looked down and saw blood running down her dress. It was her own.

Her father carried her to the trees. Her mother ran to them, tore off her scarf and pressed it over the wound, to stop the bleeding.

They didn't take any notice of what was happening on the beach, where the men stood back from the afanc, wrapped in chains, and Huw Gadarn's oxen began to pull. Slowly, slowly the afanc was dragged up the beach, and the oxen drew it away.

The stories say that this was such hard work, even for the mighty horned oxen of Huw Gadarn, that they cried as they went over the top of the hills, and the lake that was made from their tears is still there today.

The stories say that the oxen pulled the afanc all the way to the shadow of Mount Snowdon, and that when they reached the edge of the lake there, the afanc jumped in, still with the chains around it, and Huw had to work fast to free the horned oxen before they were pulled in after it.

The stories say that, even today, birds will not fly over that lake, in case the afanc rears up and pulls them down.

But the stories do not say what happened to Seren after that day. I hope she was not badly wounded, and that people still remember how brave she was.

The Three
Sisters

A TALE FROM WALES
AND ENGLAND

Once upon a time there was a king who lived in the middle of Wales. His name was Pumlumon (*you say it a bit like this: pim-lim-on*). He had three daughters: they were all brave and bold and beautiful, but quite different from each other, as sisters often are. Their names were Hafren, Gwy and Rheidol (*you say them a bit like this: Hav-ren, Gu-whee and Rhey-doll*).

Hafren was the oldest sister. She was clever and thoughtful and loved learning about the world. Her favourite hobby was reading. Gwy was the middle sister. She loved nature and knew a lot about animals, birds and fish. Her favourite thing was sitting quietly outdoors to watch and listen to the wildlife around her. Rheidol was the youngest. She loved running and dancing and turning cartwheels. Her favourite things were singing and dancing. They were all happy, living in the mountains of Wales.

One day their father the king said that he wanted to talk to them.

Hafren came to the great hall with a book in her hand. Gwy called goodbye to the birds and came indoors. Rheidol cartwheeled into the hall and nearly bumped into her father's throne. They all laughed as she turned the right way up and looked around her.

'Well, my dears,' said Pumlumon, 'it's good that you are all here. I want to talk to you about the kingdom.'

The girls looked at him in surprise.

'I'm getting old, and I think that being king is quite hard work. I didn't mind when I was young, but now I would like to stop and rest. That means someone else needs to take care of the kingdom. It is too big a job for one person, so I want you to share the land between you. And I've had an idea. Why don't you each make a journey?

Start at the top of our mountain and keep going until you reach the sea. Think about the places you like best and what things you would like to be in charge of. Share the kingdom between the three of you. What do you think?'

'It's a great idea,' cried Rheidol excitedly. 'I would like to run straight down the mountain to the sea and be in charge of the shore and the beaches!'

'It is a good idea,' said Gwy. 'I would like to wander through the countryside and take care of all the places where birds and animals gather.'

'I like it too,' said Hafren. 'I would like to go through the towns and cities and see the libraries and museums. Those are the places I would most like to look after.'

And so it was agreed. That night they were all very excited.

Hafren kept a cool head. She collected everything that she thought she would need, and checked a map. She chose her path carefully. Gwy thought about the birds and animals she loved, and looked in her nature books to find their favourite places to go through. Rheidol was so excited that she couldn't go to sleep for ages.

In the morning Hafren woke up early, picked up her things and set off. She wasn't going fast, just taking her time, looking to left and right, and enjoying the journey.

Gwy woke up soon after. She checked her nature books once more and went eagerly down the mountain, turning this way and that, and listening to the early morning birdsong.

Rheidol was still in bed. She had gone to sleep so late that now she couldn't wake up. When she did wake, the sun was already high in the sky. She jumped out of bed, pulled on her clothes and quickly washed her face and cleaned her teeth. She ran out of the palace. Her sisters were nowhere to be seen.

'Oh, I'm late!' she cried, and she ran off down the mountainside, taking the quickest way to the sea.

All day long the three sisters travelled. Hafren made sure her path led her through towns and cities. Gwy wandered here and there across the countryside. Rheidol rushed towards the shining sea.

As evening approached, the two older sisters caught sight of each other. Gwy ran to Hafren and they went on together, holding hands, until they reached the sea where Wales and England meet. Rheidol had gone down the mountain on the other side. She ran and ran, the wind in her hair, until she came to the sea on the west coast of Wales.

And that's how Hafren, Gwy and Rheidol shared the kingdom and gave their father a rest. Where the three sisters went, three rivers now flow from the top of the mountain to the sea.

Afon Hafren, called the River Severn in English, goes down the mountainside and through the towns of Newtown and Welshpool before leaving Wales and flowing into England. There the river goes through Shrewsbury, Worcester and Gloucester before it reaches the sea. It is the longest river in Britain.

Afon Gwy is called the River Wye in English. It is a Special Area of Conservation and is home to many animals, birds and fish. When it reaches the flat lands near the sea, it joins the Hafren, and they flow into the sea together.

Afon Rheidol has the same name in English and Welsh. It runs swiftly down the mountain, with some wonderful waterfalls, before it tumbles into the sea at Aberystwyth.

In the middle of Wales there is a mountain with five peaks. It is called Pumlumon; three beautiful rivers rise there and flow to the sea.

Now you know their story.

Mossycoat

A TALE FROM THE
ENGLISH GYPSY TRADITION

Once upon a time there was a girl. She lived with her mother in a little house with roses round the door. They weren't very rich and they weren't very poor. They were just fine.

One day, there was a knock on the door. When the girl opened it, a tinker was standing there.

Now, in those days and those times, the tinkers used to travel around from house to house, with small things to sell, like pegs and pins, or buttons and bows. They would mend things too.

The tinker had come to the house to find out if they wanted to buy anything. But when he saw the girl, he just fell madly in love with her!

So he said, 'Darling, will you marry me?'

Well, she didn't want to get married, and anyway, she didn't know him, but she didn't want to be rude. She didn't know what to say or do. So she did what you do when you don't know what to do. She went to ask her mum.

Her mum said, 'My dear, you don't need to worry about a thing, because I am making you a marvellous, magical *something*, and when it's done, you can go far away to seek your fortune, and you won't have to worry about the tinker at all. But it's going to take me a bit longer to finish my work, so we must find a way to make the tinker wait. I know! Tell him you will only marry him if he brings you a beautiful dress made of white satin, all covered with big sprigs of gold, as big as your hand – and the dress has got to fit you perfectly. That will take him some time to make. That will give me time to finish my work.'

The girl went back and told the tinker, and he said, 'Darling, whatever you want, I will be glad to get it for you!' And he looked at her, to see what size she was, and he went away.

The very next day, he was back, with a beautiful white dress with big sprigs of gold. The girl took it away and tried it on, and it fitted her perfectly.

'Now what shall I do?' she asked her mum.

'Well, I still need a bit longer to finish my work. Tell him you will only marry him if he brings you a beautiful dress, made of all of the colours of all of the birds of the air, and no two colours the same – and the dress has got to fit you perfectly. That will take him a bit of time. That will give me time to finish my work.'

The girl went back and told the tinker.

He said, 'Of course, my dear, whatever you want!' And he went away.

The very next day, he was back, with a beautiful dress made of all of the colours of all of the birds of the air.

The girl took it away and tried it on, and it fitted her perfectly.

'Now what shall I do?' she asked her mum.

'Well, I still need a bit longer to finish my work. Tell him you will only marry him if he brings you a pair of white silk dancing shoes – and they have to fit you perfectly! That will take him a bit of time. That will give me time to finish my work.'

The girl went back and told the tinker.

He said, 'Of course, my dear, whatever you want!' And he went away.

But the very next day, he was back, with a beautiful pair of white silk dancing shoes. And of course, they fitted her perfectly!

'Now what shall I do?' the girl asked her mum.

'My dear, you don't have to worry about a thing!' said her mum. 'Because tonight I will finish making the marvellous magical *something*, and tomorrow you will be far away from here, seeking your fortune. Tell the tinker to come back tomorrow.'

The next day, the tinker must have been very disappointed, because the girl *was* far away. That night, her mother finished the thing she was making. It was a magic wishing coat, made of golden thread and soft green moss woven together.

She gave it to her daughter and said, 'When you are wearing this coat, whatever you wish for will come true. Wish yourself a hundred miles away from here. In the blink of an eye you will be there, and you will see a big house on the top of a hill. Go to the front door and ask for work, because that is where you will find your fortune.'

The girl was sad to be leaving her mum, but excited to be going to seek her fortune. She put on the magic mossy coat, and she packed the white dress, and the colourful dress, and the satin dancing shoes – because you never know when you might be invited to a party.

Then she said goodbye to her mum and she touched the coat … and closed her eyes … and wished …

When she opened her eyes, she was in a place she had never seen before. She saw a big house on the top of a hill. She knocked on the door and asked the lady of the house for work.

The lady liked the polite way the girl spoke, so she gave her a job as the cook's assistant. The lady took her to the kitchen and introduced her to the cook.

'This girl is Mossycoat. I have given her a job as your assistant. Make her feel at home and give her a nice bedroom with a view of the lake.'

The cook smiled and curtsied and said, 'Oh, yes, Madam.'

But as soon as the lady had gone out of the kitchen, the cook stopped smiling and started to glare at Mossycoat. 'You aren't having a job as my assistant,' she said. 'I don't know you. I don't like you. You can have all the dirty pots and pans to wash. And you're not having a nice bedroom with a view of the lake. You can sleep in the cupboard under the stairs, where the boots and shoes are kept!'

Then she took down the biggest soup spoon and hit Mossycoat on the head with it. It really hurt! But Mossycoat didn't complain.

When they gave her all the dirty pots and pans, she scrubbed until they were shining. She worked hard, day after day, but the cook didn't get any kinder. Every day she hit Mossycoat on the head with the big soup spoon, and every night she pushed Mossycoat into the cupboard under the stairs. And that was where she slept.

Things went on like this for quite a while.

Then one day, the lady announced that her son was coming home. There was going to be a big party for him. Everyone in the kitchen was excited.

'We can make our favourite recipes,' they said. 'We can put out the golden cups and silver plates, and we can go up to the ballroom when our work is finished, and listen to the music and watch the people dancing.'

Then they turned to look at Mossycoat. 'But you aren't coming, Mossycoat. Your greasy hands will make the fine clothes all dirty. You can stay in the kitchen!' And the cook took down the big soup spoon and hit Mossycoat on the head.

The first night of the party came, and all the people from the kitchen went to watch the dancing. Mossycoat was left sitting in the kitchen by herself.

The next day everyone in the kitchen was chatting about the music and the dancing and the lovely clothes. Mossycoat thought, 'I would like to see the dancing.'

So that night, when everyone was working, she went round the kitchen and touched them all with her magic mossy coat. She wished they would all fall asleep. Straight away, they all fell asleep, right in the middle of the work!

So no one saw Mossycoat wish herself into the cupboard under the stairs. No one saw her wish herself clean. No one saw her change into her white silk dress and her white silk dancing shoes.

She put her magic wishing coat back on. She touched the coat and wished herself into the ballroom. When she appeared, all the people were amazed. She was so beautiful. The lady's son looked at her. When he looked at her, he liked her. Then his heart went '*Ba-boom*!' and he fell in love with her.

He went straight to her and asked her to dance with him.

Mossycoat said, 'I can only dance one dance tonight, and then I must go. But if I can only dance one dance, I would be glad to dance it with you.'

She curtsied. He bowed. The band began to play. They danced all the way up the room. They danced all the way down again. When they got near to the door, Mossycoat touched her magic mossy coat and wished herself away. In the blink of an eye, she was gone!

The young man made everyone run around to look for her. They thought they looked everywhere. But no one thought of looking in the cupboard under the stairs, where the boots and shoes were kept. That's where she was, taking off her dancing dress and dancing shoes, putting on her dirty work clothes. Then she put on her mossy coat.

She went round the kitchen touching everyone with her coat, to wake them up. When they realised they had been sleeping, instead of working, they said, 'Oh, Mossycoat, please don't tell on us. Don't get us into trouble.'

She said she would not. And for once, she did not get hit on the head with the big soup spoon.

The next day, all everyone in the kitchen wanted to talk about was the lovely lady who had danced with the young master. 'Will she come again?' they asked.

'We must all watch for her tonight,' they said.

Then they said, 'But you can't come, Mossycoat. Your greasy hands will make her fine clothes all dirty.'

Mossycoat didn't say anything, but she thought, 'If I'm not there, you won't see that lovely lady.'

So that evening, she did it all again. She made them go to sleep with her magic mossy coat. She got all dressed up. This time, she put on her colourful dress and her dancing shoes. But she kept her mossy coat on.

When she wished herself into the dance, everyone was excited to see her, the young master most of all. He went straight to her and asked her to dance with him.

Mossycoat said, 'I can only dance one dance tonight, and then I must go. But if I can only dance one dance, I would be glad to dance it with you.'

She curtsied. He bowed. The band began to play.

They danced all the way up the room. They danced all the way down again. When they got near to the door, Mossycoat touched her coat again, and wished herself away. But this time, the young man tried to hold on to her.

He must have knocked her foot as she disappeared, because when he looked around, she was gone. But there on the floor was one of her white silk dancing shoes.

He picked it up. 'Oh, where is the lovely lady who wore this shoe?' he asked. 'I must find her.'

Once again, he made everyone run around to look for her. But no one thought of looking in the cupboard under the stairs, where the boots and shoes were kept. That's where she was, taking off her dancing dress and one dancing shoe, the one she hadn't lost.

Then she put on her dirty work clothes. She put on her mossy coat too. Then she went round the kitchen touching everyone with her coat, to wake them up.

The next day, the young man was still searching for the girl who had worn the shoe. He made everyone who had been at the party try on the shoe. It didn't fit anyone. Then he made everyone who had worked at the party try on the shoe. The people from the kitchen went to try it on too.

But the cook said, 'Not you, Mossycoat. Your greasy clothes will make that fine shoe dirty.'

So Mossycoat was left in the kitchen. Everyone else tried on the shoe. It didn't fit any of them.

The young man asked the cook, 'Has everyone tried the shoe?'

'Everyone except that dirty greasy girl Mossycoat,' said the cook.

'Well, Mossycoat must try it too,' he said.

So Mossycoat was sent for. When she came, she put out her foot and tried on the shoe. It fitted her perfectly!

'Darling, I love you!' said the young man.

'Wait a minute,' said Mossycoat.

She wished herself away into the cupboard under the stairs and changed into her white silk dress. She put on her other shoe, the one she hadn't lost, and her mossy coat. Then she wished herself back again.

'You look lovely,' he said.

'Wait a minute,' she said.

She wished herself away again, and changed into her colourful dress.

When she wished herself back, he said: 'Darling, I don't care what you wear! I love you. Will you marry me?'

Well, she said she would, and when they had the wedding, her mum was invited. All the people who had been at the party were invited. Everyone had a lovely time.

When the lady heard how mean the cook had been to Mossycoat, she sent her away, and got someone kinder to work for her instead.

And I think that was fair, don't you?

The
Dauntless
Girl

A TALE FROM ENGLAND

Once there was a girl called Mary, who worked for a farmer. The farmer used to boast about Mary, 'She's not afraid of anything. She would go anywhere, do anything. She's dauntless, that one!'

His friend the blacksmith was sure he could think of something that Mary would be too afraid to do. He said, 'I bet Mary won't go to the church at midnight and bring back a skull bone from the dead house there.'

The farmer said, 'I bet she will!'

The bet was a golden coin. The blacksmith didn't want to lose his bet, so he asked the man whose job was digging the graves to hide in the dead house and give Mary a fright.

The next night, when it was nearly midnight, those two friends asked Mary, 'Will you go to the church please, and bring us back a skull bone from the dead house? As long as you aren't too scared ...'

She said, 'Well, I can't think what you want an old skull bone for, but I don't mind going. It's a nice night for a walk. I'll get my coat.'

When she came to the dead house, the gravedigger was hiding inside. Mary picked up a skull, and the gravedigger called out in a ghostly voice, 'Don't touch that skull bone. It's my father's skull bone.'

So Mary put it down and picked up another. The ghostly voice came again. 'Don't touch that skull bone. It's my mother's skull bone.'

Mary put that one down and picked up another. She was getting annoyed with the ghostly voice, so, before he could call out again, she said, 'I don't care if this skull bone belonged to your father or your mother or your sister or your brother. I must have a skull bone and I'm taking this one!'

Off she went with the skull bone, and she slammed the door of the dead house behind her. The farmer and the blacksmith were surprised to see her come back so quickly.

The blacksmith asked her, 'Mary, weren't you afraid? They say there are ghosts in the dead house.'

Mary said, 'Well, there was a silly old ghost, and every time I picked up a skull bone it said, "Don't touch that skull bone." But I told it I must have a skull bone, and I brought one home, even though it didn't like it. I could hear that old ghost moaning and groaning even after I slammed the door and came away.'

The blacksmith felt worried then. He wondered if the gravedigger was stuck in the dead house. He paid the farmer the golden coin and hurried away.

Bad news! When he opened the door of the dead house, the gravedigger was flat on the floor. He had fainted in fear. Mary became quite famous after that, as the dauntless girl who wasn't afraid of anything, even a ghost in the dead house in the middle of the night.

A young squire who lived not far away heard about Mary. Ever since his old mother died, her ghost had been troubling him: moaning in the bedrooms and groaning in the corridors, appearing in the kitchen and even trying to sit down to dinner with him. She had frightened the servants, and they had all left. The squire had no one to cook or keep house for him.

He came to see Mary. 'Would you come to work for me? I'll pay you extra, because my mother's ghost might trouble you.'

'I'm not afraid of your mother's ghost, and your wages are better than I'm getting now. Besides, I don't like people making bets about me. I'll get my coat.'

So Mary went to work in the grand house, and she liked it quite well. The ghost was always drifting around, but Mary made sure she was very polite to it. She laid a place for it at the table every meal time, and made sure that the knives and forks were not crossed, because she knew that would stop the ghost from coming near. She even offered it the dishes of vegetables when she brought them to the table.

She would ask the ghost, 'Would you like some pepper, madam? Can I pass you the salt?'

Things went on like this for a while, until the young squire went away on business. Mary was sweeping the kitchen floor when the door creaked open. Some thin wispy fog squeezed through the gap, and then spread out. It was the old lady's ghost.

The ghost had never spoken to anyone before, but it spoke to Mary now. 'Mary, you're a good girl and you treat me right. I want to show you something. Open the cellar door and come down there with me … as long as you aren't too scared. You won't need a light. I'll shine for us both.'

Mary wasn't scared at all. She opened the cellar door and followed the gleaming ghost down the steep stone steps. 'Move those bricks in the corner, Mary,' said the ghost.

Mary lifted up the bricks and saw two bags hidden underneath them.

'Mary,' said the ghost, 'that's my fortune, that I hid down here. I died before I could tell my son where it was. I've been trying to find someone to tell all this time, but you're the only one who isn't afraid of me. Give the big bag of gold to my son. You can keep the small one, to thank you for helping me.'

Then the ghost disappeared. Mary had a hard time finding her way out of the cellar again, without a light to show her the way. But she was dauntless. So she did it.

When the squire came back, Mary said to him, 'Sir, I need to show you something. Please come with me.'

She lit a candle and led him down into the cellar. 'Your mother showed me this while you were away,' she said, pointing to the two bags of gold, still lying in the corner. 'She wants you to have the little bag and me to have the big bag.'

The squire was a bit surprised that his mother hadn't given the big bag to him, but he didn't complain. He lifted up the little bag and Mary took the big bag. They carried them upstairs.

Mary was rich now, but she liked her work, so she carried on working at the squire's house. She didn't want the old ghost to come back, though, and tell the squire that he should have had the big bag. So from then on, she always crossed the knives and forks on the table, to keep the old ghost away, so it couldn't come back to tell him.

The ghost never did come back.

Mary lived happily for the rest of her days, and no one ever troubled her, because everyone knew that she wasn't afraid of anything.

The Girl Who Sang Herself to Safety

A TALE FROM SPAIN

Once upon a time, a girl and her mother lived in a little house on the edge of a small village in Spain. They were quite poor, but the girl had one treasure. It was a pretty necklace of shells that her mother had given her. She loved to wear it and always took good care of it.

The girl helped her mother as much as she could. One of her jobs was to go every day to the well in the village square to fetch water. The well was deep and the girl didn't want to lose her necklace in the water when she leaned over with her bucket. She always took it off and laid it carefully on a big stone near the well while she filled her bucket. Then she would put her necklace on again and carry the bucket home.

On the day that the story begins, the girl was leaning over the well to fill her bucket, when she heard a strange noise. She looked up.

A great big hairy monster was stomping into the square! She grabbed her bucket and ran. She ran and she ran until she was nearly home, and then she thought of something terrible!

She put her hand to her neck. Her necklace wasn't there! It was still on the stone beside the well.

She put down her bucket and tried to decide what to do. But she knew there was only one thing to do. She couldn't lose her necklace. She had to go back.

At the corner of the square, she peeped carefully round the wall. The monster was sitting on the wall of the well, holding her necklace. When it saw her, it grinned a horrible grin, and held out the necklace.

Slowly, slowly, she went towards it. When she was almost near enough to reach out and get the necklace, but still too far away for the monster to get her, she stopped.

She felt very afraid, but she gathered all her courage … suddenly, she rushed forward and grabbed the necklace.

But the monster grabbed her! Its arms were longer than she had thought. It held her up and looked at her. Its eyes were big and round, like fish eyes. It spoke to her. Its voice was gruff and slobbery. It said, 'Now I've got you, and you will work for me!'

Before the girl could say a word, the monster stuffed her into a sack and tied up the top. It put the sack on its back and lumbered away from the well. It went as far as the house on the corner and knocked on the door.

When the door was opened, the girl heard the monster say: 'I've got a singing sack. If my sack sings to you, what will you give me to eat?'

And someone answered, 'A singing sack? I've never heard of such a thing! If your sack really can sing, I'll give you some soup.'

The monster lifted the sack. It growled at the girl inside, 'Sing, singing sack, or I'll give you a whack!'

The girl trembled. She began to sing in a scared little voice:

I am my mother's only daughter,
Now I am alone, all alone, all alone.
She sent me to fetch her the water,
Now I can't go home, can't go home,
can't go home.

'That's a lovely little song!' said the person
in the house, and the girl heard the monster
slurp down a great big bowl of soup.

The monster went to the next house. It
knocked on the door. When the door was
opened, the girl heard the monster say: 'I've
got a singing sack. If my sack sings to you,
what will you give me to eat?'

And someone answered, 'A singing sack?
I've never heard of such a thing! If your sack
really can sing, I will give you some bread
and cheese.'

The monster lifted the sack. It growled
at the girl inside, 'Sing, singing sack, or I'll
give you a whack!'

The girl began to sing again.

I am my mother's only daughter,
Now I am alone, all alone, all alone.
She sent me to fetch her the water,
Now I can't go home, can't go home,
can't go home.

'That's a sad little song!' said the person in the house, and the girl heard the monster gobble up a cheese sandwich.

The monster went to the next house. And the next. And the next. At each house it made the girl sing. At each house people gave it something to eat.

The monster was very greedy. It went right through the whole village, until there was only one house left. The monster went to the last house and knocked on the door. When the door was opened, the monster said, 'I've got a singing sack. If my sack sings to you, what will you give me to eat?'

And it was the girl's mother who answered!

The girl sang her song:

I am my mother's only daughter,
Now I am alone, all alone, all alone.
She sent me to fetch her the water,
Now I can't go home, can't go home,
can't go home.

The mother recognised her daughter's voice at once. She thought quickly.

She said, 'That's lovely. I have just made supper, but my daughter hasn't come home. Why don't you come in and eat her food?'

The monster went in. It put the sack in the corner and sat at the table in the girl's place. The mother gave the monster soup and rice and meat and bread and tomatoes and fruit and wine. Soon, the monster was so full that it fell asleep with its fat piggy nose on the table. It snored really loudly.

Then the mother undid the sack and her daughter climbed out. They hugged each other.

'Shush!' said the mum, 'Don't wake it up. I've got an idea.' She fetched their cat and their dog and put them in the sack, tying it up tightly again. The cat and dog didn't like it, but they put up with it. The girl hid in a cupboard.

When the monster woke up, the mother gave it the sack and it went away. It didn't notice anything different about the sack, until it came to the first house in the next village.

The monster went to the house and knocked on the door. When the door was opened, the monster said, 'I've got a singing sack. If my sack sings to you, what will you give me to eat?'

And someone answered, 'A singing sack? I've never heard of such a thing! If your sack really can sing, I will give you some breakfast.'

The monster lifted the sack. It growled, 'Sing, singing sack, or I'll give you a whack!'

But nothing happened.

The monster shook the sack and said again, 'Sing, singing sack, or I'll give you a whack!' Still nothing happened, though the sack did wiggle a bit.

'I think your sack is broken,' sniggered the person on the doorstep, and she went back inside and shut the door.

The monster was angry. It whacked the sack. Inside the sack, the dog barked and the car miaowed. 'What kind of song is that?' growled the monster. It opened the sack.

Out jumped the cat and dog!

The cat scratched the monster on its fat piggy nose. The dog bit the monster on its fat piggy bum. Then they ran away home. The monster rubbed its nose and its bum. Then it threw the sack away and stomped off home. Wherever that was!

No one ever saw it again.

The girl and her mother heard scratching at their door. They opened the door. Their cat and their dog were waiting there. 'Well done, you two,' said the mum. 'Now we'll get some peace, I think.'

The monster never bothered them again.

And the girl still has the special necklace made of shells that her mother gave her.

Red Riding Hood

(BUT NOT AS
YOU KNOW HER!)

A TALE FROM FRANCE

Once upon a time there was a girl who lived with her mother in a little cottage on the edge of the forest. The mother baked some bread. She said to her daughter, 'Take a warm loaf and this bottle of milk to your granny.'

At the crossroads the girl met a wolf. 'Where are you going?' asked the wolf.

'I'm taking some bread and milk to my granny,' said the girl.

'Which path will you choose?' asked the wolf. 'The path of needles or the path of pins?'

'The path of needles,' said the girl.

'Then I'll take the path of pins,' said the wolf.

The girl wandered along the path she had chosen, picking up the needles as she went.

The wolf raced along the path of pins, until he came to the grandmother's house in the middle of the forest. He burst in and ate up the grandmother! He climbed into her bed and pulled the covers over his long nose.

The girl reached the cottage and knocked on the door.

'Lift up the latch and come in,' called the wolf.

The girl went in and said, 'Good morning, Granny. I've brought you a fresh loaf and a bottle of milk.'

'Put the bread and milk on the shelf, next to that bottle of wine,' said the wolf. 'And have a drink of wine if you are thirsty.'

The girl looked at the bottle. She hadn't ever drunk wine. She wondered what it was like. But then the little cat curled up by the fire hissed, 'Don't drink that!'

So she said, 'No thanks, Granny, I'm not thirsty.'

'Very well,' said the wolf. 'Take off your clothes and get into bed with me.'

The girl took off her jumper. She said, 'What shall I do with my jumper?'

The wolf said, 'Throw it into the fire, my dear. You won't need it any more.'

She took off her shoes. 'What shall I do with my shoes?'

The wolf said, 'Throw them into the fire, my dear. You won't need them any more.'

She took off her socks. 'What shall I do with my socks?'

The wolf said, 'Throw them into the fire, my dear. You won't need them any more.'

She said, 'I'm not taking off anything else, Granny. I'll be cold.'

'All right then. Get into bed with me.'

The girl got into bed. She looked at the wolf. She said, 'Oh, Granny, how hairy you are!'

'All the better to keep myself warm, my child.'

'Oh, Granny, what big nails you have!'

'All the better to scratch myself with, my child.'

'Oh, Granny, what big shoulders you have!'

'All the better to carry firewood, my child.'

'Oh, Granny, what big ears you have!'

'All the better to hear you with, my child.'

'Oh, Granny, what a big nose you have!'

'All the better to smell you with, my child.'

'Oh, Granny, what a big mouth you have!'

'All the better to gobble you up, my child.'

The girl thought fast. She had been pretty sure, all along, that this was *not* her granny. Now she knew she had to get out of there. She said, 'Oh, Granny, I need a wee!'

'Do it in the bed,' said the wolf.

'Ugh, Granny, no, that's nasty. Let me go outside and do it.'

'All right, but be quick!'

The wolf tied a rope to the girl's foot and held tight to the other end, in case she tried to run away.

The girl went outside. She tied her end of the rope to the plum tree in the yard, and ran away as fast as she could.

The wolf waited and waited. Then he got impatient. He called out, 'Why are you taking so long? Are you having a poo?'

When there was no answer, he jumped out of bed and ran into the yard. He saw that the girl had escaped. He raced after her, and followed her home, but he was too late. He got to her house just as she slammed the door. The girl and her mother were safe.

The wolf kept well away from them after that. He knew that the girl was too clever for him.

The Little Girl Sold with the Pears

A TALE FROM ITALY

Once upon a time there was a farmer who had many fields of fruit trees. Her farm belonged to the king. Every autumn, the farmer paid rent to the king. The rent was four baskets of pears.

But one year the farmer only had enough pears to fill three and a half baskets. So she asked her little daughter to climb into the fourth basket. Then she put the last few pears on top of the little girl, and the basket looked full. She took the baskets of pears to the palace and they were put in the larder.

The farmer went home. The little girl stayed in the basket. When she got hungry, she ate some pears. After a while, the servants noticed that there weren't so many pears in the baskets. They saw pips and stalks lying around. They looked in all the baskets and they found the little girl, so they took her to the king. The king said she could stay and work in the palace.

The little girl grew up in the palace. Everyone called her Perina, because they had found her in a basket of pears. She was friendly and everyone liked her.

The king's son liked her: they were the same age and they played together, even though he was a prince and she was a servant. But this made the other servants jealous, so they decided to get Perina into trouble with the king. They made up a lie and told it to the king, 'That girl boasts all the time. She says she can do anything. She says she can get the witch's treasure from the house with the dangerous door.'

'Hmm,' thought the king. 'It would be very nice to have a witch's treasure.' So he sent for Perina and said, 'I want you to bring me the witch's treasure from the house with the dangerous door.'

Perina was surprised. 'Sorry, your majesty,' she said, 'I don't know where that is.'

'I think you do!' said the king. 'So off you go, and don't come back without it.'

Perina didn't have much choice, so she left the palace. At the palace gate her friend the prince called to her. He said, 'I know what you're looking for. If you can find the witch's treasure and give it to me, it will break the spell that keeps me a prisoner in the palace. I hope you find the treasure.'

'So do I,' said Perina. She waved goodbye to the prince and began to walk.

She walked and she walked until she was tired. She came to an apple tree, but she didn't stop. She came to a cherry tree, but she didn't stop. She came to a pear tree. She climbed up into the branches and went to sleep. When she woke up, a little old woman was sitting under the tree.

The old woman said, 'I know what you're looking for. If you find the witch's treasure and give it to the prince, it will make him free. I will help you find the treasure. You will need three things and a spell to help you on your

way. Here are the three things you will need.'
She gave Perina a broom, a loaf of bread and
a pack of butter. Then she taught her a spell
and told her when she would need to use it.

Perina thanked her and went on her way.
She came to a bakery. Three women were
trying to clean it. They were sweeping the
crumbs and flour out of the oven. They were
sweeping with their hair.

'Why are you sweeping with your hair?'
asked Perina.

'Because we haven't got a broom,' they said.

'I've got a broom,' said Perina. 'You can
have it.'

'Oh, thank you!' they said. 'That is really
helpful.'

Perina gave them the broom and went on
her way. She came to a fierce red river. There
was no bridge and the river was too fast and
too deep to swim.

She knew she needed to cross the river, so
she used the old woman's spell.

She said:

Red river so fine,
I must hurry along.
Or else I would stop
To hear your song.

The river stopped running, and she was able to cross, without even getting her feet wet. When she reached the other side she turned and said:

Red river so fine,
You've been very kind.
But now I must go
There's a treasure to find.

The river started to run again and she went on her way. She climbed a hill and came to a grand gate at the beginning of a long path. Three fierce guard dogs were chained to the gate. They barked and growled at her.

'Why are you barking and growling?' asked Perina. The dogs didn't answer in words, but she could see that they were hungry. 'I've got some bread,' said Perina. 'You can have it.' She broke the loaf of bread into three pieces and threw it to the dogs.

They gobbled it all up and wagged their tails to say 'Thank you'.

She went on her way and followed the path. It led to a magnificent house. The door of the house was slamming shut and bursting open, over and over again. It looked really dangerous. It was making a horrible squeaking noise.

'Why are you squeaking so loudly?' asked Perina. The door didn't answer, of course, but she could hear that the hinges needed greasing. 'I've got some butter,' said Perina. 'You can have it.'

She rubbed the butter on the door hinges until the door stopped slamming and banging and squeaking. It opened quietly and just stayed like that.

Perina went in. In the middle of the room was a treasure chest. She picked it up and turned to go. The treasure chest started shouting, 'Door, door, slam on her. Don't let her get away!'

'I won't stop her,' said the door, 'because she greased my hinges, that no one's looked after since goodness knows when.'

Perina ran down the path and came to the gate. The treasure chest started shouting, 'Dogs, dogs, bite her. Don't let her get away!'

'We won't stop her,' said the dogs, 'because she gave us bread, when no one has fed us since goodness knows when.'

Perina ran down the hill and came to the river. The treasure chest started shouting, 'River, river, drown her. Don't let her get away!'

'I won't stop her,' said the river, 'because she called me "Red river so fine", which no one has said since goodness knows when.'

The river stopped running, and she was able to cross without even getting her feet wet.

She came to the bakery. The treasure chest started shouting, 'Women, women, catch her. Don't let her get away!'

'We won't stop her,' said the women, 'because she gave us a broom, the first one we have had since goodness knows when.'

After that, the treasure chest didn't say any more.

When she was nearly home, Perina started wondering what was in the treasure chest. Even though she knew she shouldn't, she opened the lid to have a peep. Out came a hen with all her golden chicks.

Before Perina knew it, they had all got away, too fast for her to catch them. She set out to look for them. She passed the apple tree. They weren't there. She passed the cherry tree. They weren't there. She came to the pear tree, and there was the little old woman throwing corn to the hen and the golden chicks.

'Shoo, shoo!' said the old woman, and the hen and all her chicks went back into the treasure chest. Perina closed the lid to keep them safe.

When Perina got back to the palace, the prince was waiting by the gate. He said to her, 'When my father asks you what you want for a reward, ask for the box of coal in the cellar.'

The king and all the servants were standing on the doorstep. Perina gave the king the chest with the hen and chicks.

'Ask for whatever you want as your reward,' said the king.

'I would like the box of coal in the cellar, please,' said Perina.

They brought the box of coal. When she opened it, the prince jumped out.

'Now the spell on me is broken and I can go wherever I want!' he cried. 'Thank you for rescuing me, Perina.'

And they both lived happily ever after.

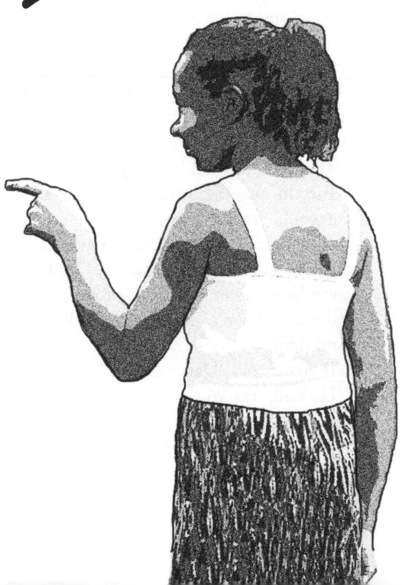

Ibanang

A TALE FROM NIGERIA

Ibanang lived in a little village with her mother and father, near to the edge of the forest. They always kept a close eye on her and wouldn't let her play out on her own, even though she said to them, 'I'm old enough now. All my friends are allowed. Why can't I? I will be careful.'

They wouldn't tell her why.

But this was the reason: they were afraid she would get lost in the forest.

One day, Ibanang's mother was at her market stall, selling vegetables. Her father came home from working in their fields, and he sat down to rest in the shade by the front door.

Ibanang said, 'Dad, can I play out?'

He said, 'Yes, you can play at the front of the house. I will watch you from here.'

Soon, Ibanang could see that her father was feeling sleepy. He had been working hard, and it was hot. After a while, she heard him start to snore.

She thought, 'This is my chance to explore!' She quietly opened the gate and went through the village. She crossed the fields. Her friends were playing there.

They called to her, 'Ibanang, come and play,' but she didn't stop. She thought, 'I don't know when I will get another chance to explore. I want to go further.' She went across the fields and came to the edge of the forest.

Two paths led into the forest. She looked at them. The one that went to the right looked hot and dusty. The one to the left seemed cool and shady. She took the left-hand path. She followed the path into the forest, and then she came to a bend. When she had gone round the bend, she saw a very strange thing. A tiny little drum was running towards her! It was beating itself with a tiny little stick and singing in a tiny little voice:

Ibanang, Ibanang,
Go back home.
Ibanang, Ibanang,
Bom, bom, bom.

She laughed and clapped her hands. 'The forest is full of amazing things,' she thought. 'Why have mum and dad never let me come here before?' She was so excited that she never listened to what the drum said, or paid attention to its warning. She went deeper into the forest.

She came to a second bend in the path. When she had gone round this bend, she saw a middle-sized drum running towards her. It was beating itself with a middle-sized stick and singing in a middle-sized voice:

Ibanang, Ibanang,
Go back home.
Ibanang, Ibanang,
Boom, boom, boom.

She laughed again. 'This is marvellous! The forest is really magical,' she thought. 'I wonder what else I will see?' She never listened to what the drum said, or paid attention to its warning. She went deeper into the forest.

She came to a third bend in the path. When she had gone round this bend, she saw a great big drum running towards her. It was beating itself with a great big stick and singing in a great big voice:

Ibanang, Ibanang,
Go back home.
Ibanang, Ibanang,
BOOOM, BOOOM, BOOOM.

She laughed once more. 'I wonder what else I will see?' She never listened to the drum, or paid attention to its warning. She went even deeper into the forest, until she came to the place where the path ended.

As she stood there wondering what to do, the branches opened to let her through, and the twigs, like fingers, beckoned to her. So she stepped off the path and began to go into the forest.

The branches opened in front of her, but they closed behind her so that there was no way back. Now, for the first time, she began to feel a bit afraid. The forest was dark, and it smelled strange. There were worrying little rustling sounds all around her. But ahead of her, it looked a bit lighter, so she went that way. The branches kept opening in front of her, but closing behind her, so that there was no way back.

She came out on the edge of a clearing. In the middle there was a huge drum. It was made from a whole tree trunk with a slit along the top, where the sound would come out when the sides were beaten with wooden beaters. As Ibanang watched, the slit at the top of the drum formed itself into a mouth.

The drum spoke to her. It said, 'Little girl, don't you know that everyone who comes into the heart of the forest belongs to me?' Then the wooden lips of the drum began to stretch out towards her. It opened its slit of a mouth wider and wider. It swallowed her!

Ibanang was lifted up, up, up and dropped down, down, down into the belly of the drum. At first it was too dark to see anything, but as her eyes got used to the dim light, she realised that there were people sitting in the drum. Many people. She turned to an old woman sitting next to her. 'Who are all these people?' she asked.

'We are the prisoners of the giant swallowing drum,' said the old woman. 'As long as the wooden heart of the drum is beating, we can never be free.' She pointed upwards.

Ibanang looked up, and next to the slit in the top of the drum she could see a great wooden heart hanging. It was beating: *bu-boom, bu-boom, bu-boom.*

'Have you been here long?' asked Ibanang.

'Some of us have been here for years,' said the old woman.

When she heard that, Ibanang began to cry.

And we must leave her there, for a little while, and go back to the house in the village, where her father was sleeping on a chair in the doorway.

Ibanang's mother came home, and that woke up the father. 'Where's Ibanang?' asked the mum.

'She's playing at the front of the house,' said the dad.

'No, she isn't,' said the mum. 'I just came in that way. I didn't see her.'

They looked round the back of the house. They looked inside the house. They couldn't find Ibanang anywhere.

Ibanang's mother had a bad feeling. She ran through the village until she came to the fields. She called to the children playing there. 'Have you seen my daughter? Have you seen Ibanang?'

'She did come past,' the children called back. 'But she didn't stop. She went that way.' They pointed towards the forest.

Ibanang's mother ran on, until she came to the edge of the forest. She looked at the two paths leading into the forest, one to the left and one to the right. She looked at the right-hand path. She couldn't see anything. She looked at the left-hand path. She saw something on the ground. It was a hair tie. She picked it up. She knew it straight away. She had put it in Ibanang's hair that morning.

Now she knew where Ibanang was, and what had happened to her. But she didn't panic or scream or cry. She turned around and went straight back into the middle of the village.

In the centre of the village, she stopped and called out. 'My friends, I need your help. My daughter has gone into the forest and she has been captured by the giant swallowing drum. I am going to rescue her. Please help me! I need you to lend me any tools that you have that can chop or cut wood.'

The people ran to look in their sheds and barns and houses. They brought out axes and saws and chisels and knives. They piled them up in a big heap in front of Ibanang's mother. She got a rope and tied the tools around her waist or hung them round her neck. She wrapped a lappa (like a cotton shawl) around herself so that all the tools were hidden.

She went out of the village and across the fields, until she came to the edge of the forest. She looked at the two paths leading into the forest. She took the left-hand one, and followed it deep into the forest. She walked until she came to the place where the path ended. The branches opened to let her through, and the twigs, like fingers, beckoned to her. She stepped off the path and into the forest. The branches opened in front of her, but they closed behind her so that there was no way back.

She came out on the edge of the clearing. In the middle was the giant swallowing drum. The slit at the top of the drum formed itself into a mouth. The drum said, 'Hey, big woman, don't you know that everyone who comes into the heart of the forest belongs to me?' The lips of the drum stretched out and swallowed her.

Ibanang's mother was lifted up, up, up and dropped down, down, down into the belly of the drum. As soon as she was inside the drum, she called out her daughter's name. Ibanang was so happy to hear her mother's voice. She ran to her and hugged and hugged her.

The other prisoners were happy too when the mother unwrapped her lappa and they saw the tools she had brought. Then they climbed up on each other's shoulders, until the one at the top was close enough to touch the great wooden heart of the drum, where it hung beating: *bu-boom, bu-boom, bu-boom.*

The others passed the sharpest axe up to the woman at the top. She chopped at the heart. It gave a great '*Bu-BOOOM*'. She chopped a second time. Again it boomed: '*Bu-BOOOM*'. She chopped a third time. This time the heart was silent.

Then they all chopped and cut at the heart, until it fell down in tiny pieces like matchsticks. After that, they cut a hole in the side of the drum. The young ones helped the old, and the strong ones helped the weak, and they all climbed out to freedom.

The prisoners of the giant swallowing drum thanked Ibanang's mother for saving them. They promised to come to see her, and to bring their families to thank her. Then they all went back to their villages.

Ibanang and her mother went home to their village. When they told the people what had happened, they went into the forest with axes and saws. They chopped up the giant swallowing drum and brought it home for firewood.

That night there was a great bonfire and a celebration, because everyone knew that they no longer had to be afraid of going into the forest. The giant swallowing drum was gone forever, thanks to Ibanang's curiosity and her mother's bravery.

Clever Ildiko

A TALE FROM HUNGARY

There was once a mayor who lived with his daughter in a little village in Hungary. He was so contented that he put a sign on his gate:

Here lives the mayor,
With his daughter Ildiko,
He hasn't any troubles,
No, no, no.

Unfortunately, when the king heard about this, he didn't like it. 'Why should he have an easy life when I have so many things to trouble me?' thought the king. So he decided to give the mayor some trouble!

He sent the mayor an old clay jug with a big hole in it, and ordered him to mend it. 'And if you don't mend it, I will have your head chopped off!'

The mayor could see that if he tried to mend the jug, it would fall to bits. He didn't know what to do. He was very scared, but his daughter Ildiko told him not to worry. 'Send the jug back to the king and ask him to turn it inside out, so you can mend it without spoiling the pattern,' she told her father.

So that's what he did. Of course, the king could not turn the jug inside out, so he had to leave the mayor in peace … until he had another nasty idea.

He sent the mayor a wheel, and ordered him to take off its skin. 'And if you don't skin it, I will have your head chopped off!'

The mayor knew that a wheel doesn't have any skin. And he knew the king knew that too. It was clear that the king didn't want him to succeed.

But Ildiko had other ideas. 'Send the wheel back to the king, father,' she said, 'and ask him to have it killed, so that you can skin it. No one can skin an animal before it is killed. Tell him that the same must be true for wheels.'

Of course, the king could not kill the wheel, so he had to leave the mayor in peace … until he had a third nasty idea.

He invited the mayor to the palace. The mayor was very excited. He thought he was going to get a reward for being clever. Instead, the king asked him, 'Who solved my riddles?'

'My daughter, Ildiko, your majesty,' said the mayor. 'She is very clever.'

'We'll soon see how clever she is,' said the king spitefully. 'Tell her to come to the palace tomorrow. She must not wear clothes, but she must not be naked. She must not walk, but she must not ride. She must bring me a present, but she must not give me a present. If she cannot do exactly what I want, your head will be chopped off!'

The mayor went home in despair. He was sure that the next day would be his last. But Ildiko laughed. 'Cheer up, father,' she said, 'don't let our stupid king worry you. I solved his first two riddles. I can solve this one too.'

The next morning, Ildiko got up early. She went to see the neighbours on one side. They were fisherfolk, and she asked them to lend her a fishing net. She wrapped herself in the net. 'Good, now I'm not wearing clothes, but I'm not naked either,' she thought.

She went to the neighbours on the other side, who were farmers, and asked if she could borrow one of their goats. She tried sitting on its back. It was such a small goat that her feet touched the ground. 'Good, now I'm not walking, but I'm not riding either,' she thought.

She went back to her house and put out some crumbs on the bird table. When a dove came down to eat, she caught it. 'Don't be afraid, little one,' she said to the dove. 'I won't hurt you. And I won't let the king hurt you either. I need to take him a present. But I won't give you to him, I promise.'

Dressed in the net, sitting on the goat's back with her feet on the ground on each side, holding the goat's reins in one hand and carrying the dove in the other, she arrived at the palace. When she was face to face with the king, she held out the dove to him and opened her hand. The bird flew away.

'Your majesty,' she said, 'I brought you a dove as a present, but I haven't given it to you. I am not wearing clothes, but I am not naked. I am not walking, but I am not riding either. Are you satisfied now?'

The king was so surprised that he couldn't say a word.

'Please don't bother my father and me any more,' said Ildiko. 'We have a lot of important things to do.' And with that, she turned around and went home.

The king never bothered them again, because he knew that Ildiko was cleverer than he was.

Vasilisa

A TALE FROM RUSSIA

If you were Russian, I wouldn't need to tell you anything about the Baba Yaga, because she is as famous in Russia as Cinderella is here. But because you aren't in Russia, maybe you do need to know a bit about the Baba Yaga.

The Baba Yaga has beady little eyes, a great big hooked nose that nearly meets her sharp pointed chin, and iron teeth that make a sound like pokers and tongs falling down the chimney, when she gnashes them together. She has a great big barrel chest and a skinny little bottom, long bony legs and great big flat feet.

She lives in a hut in the middle of the Russian forest. The hut stands on chicken's legs, so that, whichever way you come towards it, it can turn around and see you coming with its great big window eyes. Around the hut is a fence made of leg bones.

The gate is made of arm bones, with a bony hand for a latch. On the top of each fence bone is a skull. At night, when it gets dark, the eye holes in the skulls burn with a fierce red light, so that the Baba Yaga can see everything all around.

Do you want to know what her favourite food is? Her favourite food is YOU! Because the Baba Yaga is a witch …

She doesn't travel on a broomstick. That isn't how witches do things in Russia. She flies through the air in a big stone bowl, and she uses a wooden paddle to push it along. Behind her she drags a broom made of birch twigs, to sweep away her tracks so that no one can find her. Unless she wants them to.

Vasilisa was a little girl who lived at the edge of the forest. When her story begins, it is very sad, because her mother was dying.

Vasilisa sat beside her mother's bed and her mother said to her, 'Dear child, soon I will leave you. But here is a doll I have made for you. Keep her always beside you. Keep her hidden. If you need help, give her food and tell her all your troubles. She will help you. She is my blessing to you. She will help you when I cannot.'

Vasilisa took the little doll from her mother and put it in her pocket. Then she cried bitter tears. Soon after that, her mother died. Vasilisa and her father were left all alone in their house at the edge of the forest.

After a long time, or maybe a short time, Vasilisa's father decided to marry again. He thought that his new wife would be like a mother to his little girl, and her two daughters would be like sisters to Vasilisa. But he was wrong.

The new mother, I'm sorry to say, did not like Vasilisa. She was jealous of her. She thought that Vasilisa was the father's favourite, that whenever there were presents it was always Vasilisa who got the best present; whenever there were treats, it was always Vasilisa who got the nicest treat …

She was horrible to Vasilisa and told her daughters to be horrible to their new sister too. They gave Vasilisa all the hard work to do. But her doll helped her. Each night she would save some crumbs from her own food and, when she was alone, she would take her little doll from her pocket, feed it and tell it all her troubles. The doll would say to her, 'Don't worry, Vasilisa, I will help you.'

The doll did help Vasilisa. It was her friend, when there was no one else to be her friend. It did her work. It looked after her.

One day, Vasilisa's father had to go travelling. The new mother decided to get rid of Vasilisa once and for all, so that her own daughters would have the best of everything. She called the three girls to her and said, 'There is work to do and you must work until it is all done.'

To her older daughter she gave wool and a spindle and said, 'You must spin and spin until it is done.' To her younger daughter she gave wool and knitting needles and said, 'You must knit and knit until it is done.' To Vasilisa she gave silk thread and a needle and said, 'You must stitch and stitch until it is done.'

The girls worked all day, but when darkness fell, they had not finished. So they lit a candle to work by. But the candle was small, and soon it was all burned away.

The older girl said, 'I can see to do my spinning by the light of the moon.'

The younger girl said, 'I can see to do my knitting by the light of the moon.'

Then they both said, 'But you, Vasilisa, with your teeny tiny needle and teeny tiny stitches, you cannot see to finish your work. You must go to our aunt who lives in the middle of the forest and ask her for a light.'

Vasilisa started to say, 'I didn't know we have an aunt who lives in the middle of the forest …'

But before she could finish, they opened the door and pushed her out into the cold night, just as their mother had told them to do.

Vasilisa stood in the darkness. She didn't have her warm coat, or gloves, or boots. But the door was closed behind her. She put her hand in her pocket and touched the little doll, and, feeling braver because the doll was with her, she set off into the forest.

She walked all night. When the sky was just beginning to get light, a horseman all dressed in white galloped past her on a white horse. The day began.

She kept walking. A horseman all dressed in red galloped past her on a red horse. The sun rose.

She kept walking. What else could she do? She walked all day. As the day ended, a horseman all dressed in black galloped past her on a black horse. Night fell. It was dark in the forest.

But ahead of her in the darkness, Vasilisa could see a red glow. It was shining from the eye holes of skulls, on a fence of bones, surrounding a little hut which turned round and round on chicken's legs. It was the Baba Yaga's house.

Vasilisa was very afraid. But she squeezed the little doll in her pocket and that made her bold. She lifted up the bony latch on the gate and pushed it open. She went into the Baba Yaga's yard. As she stood there, wondering whether to knock on the door, there was a rushing sound behind her. She turned around to see a big bowl coming down from the sky, with a paddle pushing it along, as if it were a rowing boat in the sea. In it was the Baba Yaga.

Now Vasilisa was even more afraid. But she held tight to the little doll in her pocket.

The Baba Yaga said, 'Who are you and what do you want?'

Vasilisa answered politely, 'Good evening to you, Grandmother. I am Vasilisa. My sisters have sent me to ask you to give us a little light, so that we can see to finish our work.'

'Hmm, have they now?' said the Baba Yaga. 'Well, if you want something from me, you must do something for me. Come in, and we will see what you can do.'

They went into the Baba Yaga's hut. There was a big pot of soup bubbling on the fire. 'I'm hungry,' said the Baba Yaga. 'Serve my supper.'

Vasilisa put some soup into a bowl and the Baba Yaga gobbled it up.

'I'm still hungry,' she said. 'Give me some more.'

Vasilisa put out more soup, and more. When the Baba Yaga had finished the whole big pot full, she rubbed her belly, burped, and said: 'You can have what is left. Then wash up and tidy up. You can sleep by my fire, and in the morning, while I am away, you must sweep my house, wash my clothes, cook my food and pick out all the stones that have got mixed into my wheat store. If I am pleased with what you do, I will give you what you need.'

And without saying another word, the Baba Yaga rolled herself up in her blankets and started to snore.

Vasilisa scraped the last few spoonfuls of soup out of the bottom of the pot and into a bowl. When she was sure that the Baba Yaga was asleep, she took the little doll out of her pocket and gave it half the soup.

She whispered to her little doll, 'I'm scared. What shall I do?'

'Eat, then sleep, Vasilisa,' said the doll. 'The morning is wiser than the evening. Don't worry. I will help you do the Baba Yaga's work.'

So Vasilisa tried her best to sleep by the Baba Yaga's flickering fire. She was woken in the morning by a rushing sound, as the Baba Yaga paddled her great bowl away into the sky.

Vasilisa looked around. The work was all done! The doll had done everything while she slept. Even the stones were in a neat pile beside the wheat store. All Vasilisa had to do was rest, and cook food in time for the Baba Yaga's return.

As the day ended, the horseman dressed in black rode by, and night fell. Back came the Baba Yaga. She looked around her tidy hut, poked her long nose into the wheat store and sucked her teeth. Vasilisa put a great steaming bowl of food in front of her. The Baba Yaga grunted. 'You have done well, little one.' Then she gave a shrill whistle, and three pairs of hands with no bodies appeared in front of her.

'Grind my wheat!' she ordered, and the hands disppeared with the wheat store held between them.

Vasilisa stared and stared, but the doll jiggled about in her pocket, to warn her to keep quiet. So she did.

When the Baba Yaga had finished her huge meal, she spoke to Vasilisa. 'You have done well today, so now you can ask me a question.'

Vasilisa shyly said, 'Grandmother, when I was on my way to your house, three riders went past me. Who are they?'

The Baba Yaga said, 'The rider in white is my Bright Day. The rider in red is my

Warm Sun. And the rider in black is my Dark Night. Do you want to ask any more questions?'

Vasilisa thought of the strange hands. She opened her mouth to ask what they were, but the doll jiggled about in her pocket, to warn her to keep quiet. She said, 'No thank you, Grandmother, I have asked enough questions.'

'Hmm,' said the Baba Yaga. 'It's good that you did not ask about my servants. What happens here in my house is nobody's business but mine. Now, tomorrow you must clean and wash and cook once more, and also pick the dust out of my store of poppy seeds. When that is all done, I will give you the light you need.'

Then the Baba Yaga rolled over and began to snore.

Again Vasilisa quietly fed her little doll, and again the doll said, 'Don't worry, Vasilisa. I will help you with the work. Go to sleep now. The morning is wiser than the evening.'

When Vasilisa woke, the doll had already done all the work, and so she was able to rest until it was time to cook supper for the Baba Yaga.

When the Baba Yaga had eaten another huge meal, she whistled for the strange hands and sent them away to crush the clean poppy seeds for their oil. Then she squinted at Vasilisa with her beady little eyes.

'Somehow you have done all my work. What makes you so clever?'

Vasilisa answered, 'I am not clever, Grandmother. It is my mother's blessing that helps me.'

And she showed her little doll to the Baba Yaga. The Baba Yaga shrieked, 'A blessing? We want no blessings here! Take your blessing and your light and get out of my house!'

Well, Vasilisa was glad to go, so this was no hardship. The Baba Yaga bustled her out into the yard and grabbed one of the skulls from the fence. Its eye holes burned with a fierce red light. 'Here is your light. Take it and go!' said the Baba Yaga, and pushed Vasilisa towards her bony gate.

Vasilisa went out into the forest, carrying the skull on its long leg bone. Its red eyes lit up the path for her. She walked all night, until the white horseman passed her. It began to get light. Then the red horseman rode past, and the sun rose. The light in the skull went out, but Vasilisa carried it carefully all the way home. It was getting dark again by the time she saw her house in the distance.

When she knocked on the door the two sisters flung it open. They were wearing every coat and scarf they owned. 'We are freezing!' they moaned. 'Since you left we have not been able to light a candle or start a fire. Have you brought the light?'

'I have,' said Vasilisa, and as she spoke, the eye holes in the skull began to burn with bright fire once more. The two sisters squealed and hid their eyes. Their mother pushed past them and grabbed at the skull. But it burned her hands, and she dropped it. Flames from it rushed across the carpet and up the curtains. Vasilisa ran out of the house, but nobody followed her. The house, and everyone in it, burned up in a fierce and flaming fire.

When Vasilisa's father came home from his travels, his house was gone. His own dear daughter was staying with a neighbour. Her doll was the only thing that the fire had not destroyed. He hugged his daughter, and when he heard all that had happened to her, he promised he would not go away without her again. They built a new house and lived there together, as happy as could be.

And somewhere in the forest, the Baba Yaga chuckled.

Notes About the Stories and Where I Found Them

1. THE GIRL WHO FOUND THE STORIES

My friend the storyteller June Peters told me this story years ago, and I have loved telling it ever since. I only discovered where it comes from quite recently, when I found it in the book *Songs My Paddle Sings*, by Jim Riordan. It is a First Nation story from North America.

2. TIPINGI

I learned this story from my friend, storyteller Tony Aylwin. It is in a book of stories from Haiti collected by Diane Wolkstein. Haiti is a country on one of the islands in the Caribbean. It has many brilliant folk stories, which Diane's book helped to make well known around the world.

3. THE GIRL WHO WASN'T AFRAID

This story is new to me, and I have only just started telling it. I wanted to find an Irish story to include in this book, and I like this bold girl a lot. My version is based on one collected by Henry Glassie in *The Penguin Book of Irish Folktales*, with elements from a story I heard the Irish storyteller Susanna Steele tell years ago.

4. MOLLY WHUPPIE

I have been telling Molly Whuppie's story for a long time, and I knew I had it in a book somewhere, but I had to search my bookshelf before I found it, in Jane Yolen's *Favourite Folktales from Around the World*. She calls it an English story, but I have always thought it was from Scotland, and there is a version in which Molly has a Scots

Gaelic name, in John Francis Campbell's *Popular Tales of the West Highlands.*

5. SEREN

This is a story from North Wales. You can find it in W. Jenkyn Thomas's *The Welsh Fairy Book.*

6. THE THREE SISTERS

My friend storyteller Amy Douglas tells this story, and she put it in her first collection of stories from Shropshire, in England.

I said to her, 'But it's a Welsh story, the rivers rise in Wales.'

She said, 'But the Severn comes through Shropshire.'

You can find her version of this story in her book *Shropshire Folk Tales.* You will have to decide for yourself whether it is a Welsh story or an English one!

7. MOSSYCOAT

This is a sister story of *Cinderella*, as you probably guessed. It's one of my favourite Cinderella tales, and I tell it a lot. It's an English Gypsy version. Tinkering was one of the jobs the Gypsies used to do as they travelled around. People often say they feel sorry for the tinker and ask me what happened to him. I'm afraid I don't know his story, only Mossycoat's. You can find Mossycoat's story in *The Penguin Book of English Folktales*, edited by Neil Philip.

8. THE DAUNTLESS GIRL

This is the story that gave me the idea for this book. Like 'Mossycoat', it is in *The Penguin Book of English Folktales*.

9. THE GIRL WHO SANG HERSELF TO SAFETY

This story from Spain is in a book of stories with songs collected by storyteller Helen East, called *The Singing Sack*. You can hear the original song on the CD included with her book. My version of the song is a bit simpler, because I am not very good at singing!

10. RED RIDING HOOD

This French version of the well-known story of a little girl and a wolf is included by Angela Carter in *The Virago Book of Fairy Tales*. It is just a note (at the back of her book, on p. 241) to the much better-known story made famous by Charles Perrault. Angela Carter introduced it like this: 'This little girl, colour of clothing unknown, is not an awful warning but an example of quick thinking.'

That's why I like it.

11. THE LITTLE GIRL SOLD WITH THE PEARS

The novelist Italo Calvino published a wonderful collection of folktales from his motherland, Italy. This is my favourite story in his book, though I must admit I haven't read every story he included.

12. IBANANG

When I first got interested in storytelling, about thirty years ago, I used to go to workshops exploring stories with storytellers Mary Medlicott and Karen Tovell, and that is where and when I first heard 'Ibanang'. I didn't like it to start with, because I thought the swallowing drum was horrible. But the story grew on me, and now I tell it a lot, and I really like this story of a brave girl and her even braver mother. I have never found it in a book, though I am sure there must be collections which include it.

13. CLEVER ILDIKO

I wanted to include a story called 'The wise little girl' in this book, because I really like it. The one I know is Russian, but I already had a Russian story, 'Vasilisa'. Then the storyteller Janet Dowling sent me a weblink to some Hungarian folk tales. I found a story called 'The mayor's clever daughter' in that collection, and as it is a Hungarian version of 'The wise little girl', I decided to include it. I have given the mayor's clever daughter the name of one of my Hungarian friends.

14. VASILISA

I love stories about Baba Yaga, and this is one of the most famous. It is in Aleksandr Afanasiev's collection of fairy tales from Russia, where you can also find other Baba Yaga stories.

Further Reading

Here are some books where you can find other versions of the stories in *Folk Tales for Bold Girls*:

Aleksandr Afanasiev, *Russian Fairy Tales* (Pantheon, 1945)

Italo Calvino, *Italian Folktales* (Penguin, 1982)

John Francis Campbell, *Popular Tales of the West Highlands*, Volume 1 (Edmonston & Douglas, 1890)

Angela Carter, *The Virago Book of Fairy Tales* (Virago, 1991)

Amy Douglas, *Shropshire Folk Tales* (The History Press, 2011)

Helen East (ed.), *The Singing Sack: 28 Song-Stories from Around the World* (A & C Black, 1989)

Henry Glassie (ed.), *The Penguin Book of Irish Folktales* (Penguin, 1993)

Neil Philip (ed.), *The Penguin Book of English Folktales* (Penguin, 1991)

James Riordan, *Songs My Paddle Sings* (Chrysalis Children's Books, 1996)

W. Jenkyn Thomas, *The Welsh Fairy Book* (Dover, 2001)

Diane Wolkstein, *The Magic Orange Tree and Other Haitian Folktales* (Pantheon, 1997)

Jane Yolen (ed.), *Favourite Folktales from Around the World* (Pantheon, 1986)

Society *for*
Storytelling

Since 1993, The Society for Storytelling has championed the ancient art of oral storytelling and its long and honourable history – not just as entertainment, but also in education, health, and inspiring and changing lives. Storytellers, enthusiasts and academics support and are supported by this registered charity to ensure the art is nurtured and developed throughout the UK.

Many activities of the Society are available to all, such as locating storytellers on the Society website, taking part in our annual National Storytelling Week at the start of every February, purchasing our quarterly magazine Storylines, or attending our Annual Gathering – a chance to revel in engaging performances, inspiring workshops, and the company of like-minded people.

You can also become a member of the Society to support the work we do. In return, you receive free access to Storylines, discounted tickets to the Annual Gathering and other storytelling events, the opportunity to join our mentorship scheme for new storytellers, and more. Among our great deals for members is a 30% discount off titles from The History Press.

For more information, including how to join, please visit

www.sfs.org.uk